MICHAEL DAHL PRESENTS

SUPER FUNNY
JOKE BOOKS

WISE
CRACKERS

RIDDLES AND JOKES ABOUT
NUMBERS, NAMES, LETTERS,
AND SILLY WORDS

PICTURE WINDOW BOOKS
a capstone imprint

MICHAEL DAHL PRESENTS SUPER FUNNY JOKE BOOKS

are published by Picture Window Books
a Capstone Imprint
151 Good Counsel Drive, P.O. Box 669
Mankato, Minnesota 56002
www.capstonepub.com

Alphabet Soup and *Funny Talk* were previously published
by Picture Window Books, copyright © 2004
Chitchat Chuckles, Mind Knots, and *Nutty Names*
were previously published by Picture Window Books, copyright © 2006
Laughing Letters and Nutty Numerals and *What's in a Name?*
were previously published by Picture Window Books, copyright © 2007

Library of Congress Cataloging-in-Publication data
is available on the Library of Congress website.
ISBN: 978-1-4048-6102-2 (library binding)
ISBN: 978-1-4048-6373-6 (paperback)

Art Director: KAY FRASER
Designer: EMILY HARRIS
Production Specialist: JANE KLENK

TABLE OF CONTENTS

NUTTY NAMES:
NAME JOKES

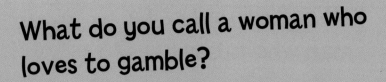

What do you call a woman who loves to gamble?

Betty.

What do you call a girl with a golden tan?

Amber.

What do you call a man who loves to work on old cars?

Rusty.

What do you call a
man who raises bees?

Buzz.

What do you call a girl who wakes
up before the sun rises?

Dawn.

What do you call a girl who lives
on a narrow street in the middle
of the block?

Alley.

What do you call a girl who likes to touch all of the animals at the zoo?

Pat.

What do you call a woman who is good at fixing flat tires?

Erin.

What do you call a boy who is good at mending clothes?

Taylor.

What do you call a boy who sits on top of a present?

Bo.

What do you call a woman who is always happy and cheerful?

Mary.

What do you call a boy
who is very tall?

Miles.

What do you call a boy who lies
in the sun all day?

Tanner.

What do you call a girl who hangs
on the mantle at Christmastime?

Holly.

What do you call a boy who loves to eat cheese dip?

Chip.

What do you call a boy who likes to jump rope?

Skip.

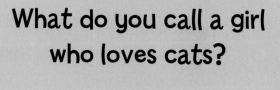

What do you call a girl who loves cats?

Kitty.

What do you call a boy who loves to throw things?

Chuck.

What do you call a boy who writes on the wall?

Mark.

What do you call a girl who has very pink cheeks?

Rosie.

What do you call
a boy who lives
in a tree?

Leif.

What do you call a boy who
has a very loud voice?

Mike.

What do you call a girl who has
words on her front and on
her back?

Paige.

What do you call a man who takes other people's things?

Rob.

What do you call a woman who is worth a lot of money?

Jewel.

What do you call a boy who can't draw very well on his own?

Trace.

WHAT DO YOU CALL A BOY WHO GIVES AWAY A LOT OF MONEY?

What do you call a girl who stands with a foot on each side of the river?

Bridget.

What do you call a girl who lives in France?

Paris.

What do you call a girl who scoops up fish?

Annette.

What do you call a man who drives a big car that carries lots of passengers?

Van.

What do you call a boy who runs after people all the time?

Chase.

What do you call a woman who loves rainy weather?

Misty.

What do you call a
boy who plays in
a pile of leaves?

Russell.

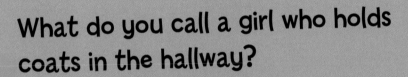

What do you call a girl who holds
coats in the hallway?

Peg.

What do you call a boy who lifts
a car with his head?

Jack.

What do you call a camel with no humps?

Humphrey.

What do you call a guy who stands in a deep hole?

Doug.

What do you call a boy who sits in a bowl?

Stu.

What do you call
a girl standing
in the distance?

Dot.

What do you call a girl who
lives on the beach?

Sandy.

What do you call a girl who
wears just one shoe?

Eileen.

What do you call a boy who lays on the grass each morning?

Dewey.

What do you call a boy who has a seagull nesting on his head?

Cliff.

What do you call a boy who is covered in fur?

Harry.

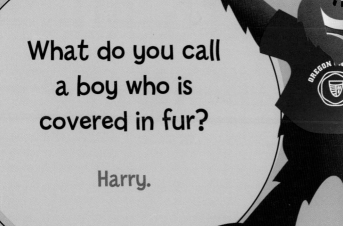

WHAT DO YOU CALL A BOY WHO SCRIBBLES PICTURES ALL OVER THE WALL?

DREW.

What do you call a boy who likes putting numbers together?

Adam.

What do you call a girl who always thinks of other people's feelings?

Karen.

What do you call a boy who sleeps by the front door?

Matt.

What do you call
a boy who is
always first?

Juan.

What do you call a pesky girl who
buzzes around your head?

Nat.

What do you call
a boy who likes to
workout?

Jim.

What do you call a girl who comes around every summer?

June.

What do you call a boy who has eight arms?

Hans.

What do you call a boy who floats in the water?

Bob.

MIND KNOTS:
SILLY RIDDLES

What is the world's laziest mountain?

Mount Everest.

What travels around the world but stays in one corner?

A postage stamp.

What can you hold without touching?

Your breath.

What did the puppy say when it climbed on top of the house?

"Roof!"

What kind of ship never sinks?

Friendship.

What kind of fur do you get from a skunk?

As fur away as possible!

How many chickens can you put in an empty box?

One. After that, the box isn't empty anymore!

What do whales like to chew?

Blubber gum.

Why were the suspenders arrested?

For holding up the pants.

What did the envelope say
to the stamp?

"Stick with me, and we'll go places."

What goes up when the
rain comes down?

Umbrellas.

Why don't bananas go sunbathing?

Because they always peel.

What kind of bow cannot be tied?

A rainbow.

What can you break with just a whisper?

Silence.

How much is a skunk worth?

A scent.

What do elves learn in school?

The elfabet.

What has lots of teeth but cannot eat?

A comb.

Where do polar bears go to dance?

A snowball.

Why did the clock get sick?

It was run down.

What kind of coat
can't be worn?

A coat of paint.

What kind of ring is always square?

A boxing ring.

What did the mother broom say to the baby broom?

"Go to sweep, baby."

What does a baby computer call its father?

Data.

What did the jack say to the car?

"May I give you a lift?"

What did the rug say to the floor?

"Don't move! I've got you covered!"

HOW DO YOU CATCH A SCHOOL OF FISH?

WITH A BOOKWORM.

What did the wall say
to the other wall?

"Meet me at the corner."

What did the muffin say
to the loaf of bread?

"Must be nice having
all that dough."

What did the baby porcupine say to the cactus?

"Mommy?"

Why did the girl sit on the watch?

She wanted to be on time.

What did the egg say to the stand-up comic?

"You crack me up!"

What did the honey bee say to the rose?

"Hi there, bud!"

What did one strawberry say to the other strawberry?

"We're in a jam."

What did the blanket say to the bed?

"Don't worry, I've got you covered."

What did the firecracker say to the other firecracker?

"My pop is bigger than your pop!"

What did one pig say to the other pig?

"Let's be pen pals."

What did the dirt say to the rain?

"If this keeps up, my name will be mud."

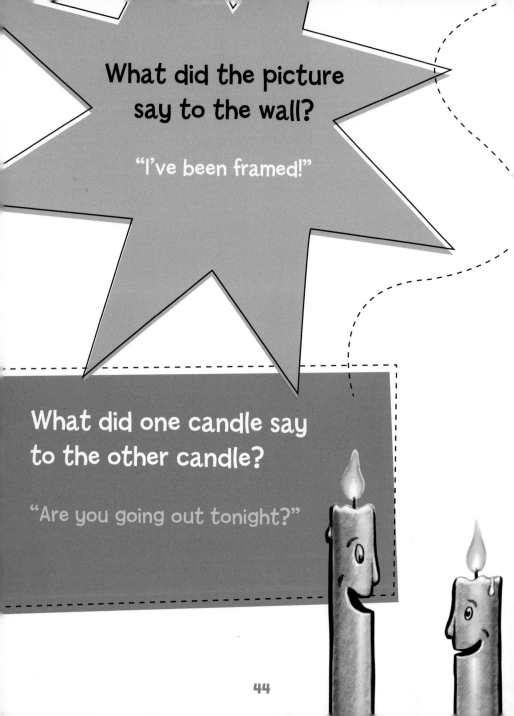

What did the picture say to the wall?

"I've been framed!"

What did one candle say to the other candle?

"Are you going out tonight?"

What did the sock say to the foot?

"You're putting me on!"

What did the second hand say to the number twelve?

"I'll be back in a minute."

What did the nose say to the finger?

"Pick on someone your own size!"

What did one raindrop say to the other raindrop?

"Two's company, three's a cloud."

What did the hammer say to the board?

"I just broke a nail!"

What did the number five say to the number seven?

"You are two much!"

What did the tie say to the hat?

"You go on a head, and I'll hang around for a while."

What did the magician say when the left side of his body disappeared?

"I'm all right now."

What did the farmer say after he dug two holes in the ground?

"Well, well."

What do volcanoes say on Valentine's Day?

"I lava you!"

What has four legs but can't walk?

A table.

What did the police officer say to his stomach?

"You're under a vest!"

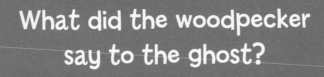

What did the woodpecker say to the ghost?

"You scared the peck out of me!"

What did the doe say to her little fawn?

"Hello, dear."

WHAT DID THE MOTHER
EARTHWORM SAY
TO HER LITTLE
EARTHWORM?

What did one angel say
to the other angel?

"Halo!"

What did the cherry say when
it was made into jam?

"This is the pits!"

What did the nut say
when it sneezed?

"Cashew!"

What did the baby porcupine say to the pin cushion?

"Mommy!"

What does Santa say when he works in his garden?

"Hoe, hoe, hoe!"

What did one flea say to the other flea?

"Shall we walk or take the greyhound?"

What did the nose say to the eyes?

"Sorry, but I gotta run!"

What did the mama cow say to her calf one night?

"Pasture bedtime, isn't it?"

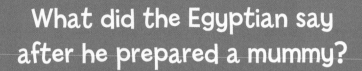

What did the Egyptian say after he prepared a mummy?

"That's a wrap!"

What did the hair say to the comb?

"Nothing can keep us apart."

What did one spider say to the other?

"See you on the web."

What did the bus driver say
to the kangaroo?

"Hop in."

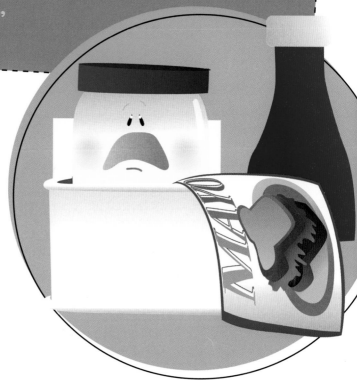

What did the mayonnaise say
to the refrigerator?

"Close the door! I'm dressing!"

What did one elevator say to the other elevator?

"I think I'm coming down with something."

What did the mother horse say to the mother goat?

"How are the kids?"

What did the invisible man's girlfriend say to him?

"I can't see you anymore."

WHAT DID THE COMPUTER SAY TO THE VIRUS?

LAUGHING LETTERS AND NUTTY NUMERALS:
NUMBER AND LETTER JOKES

To: Sarah

What letters did A and B buy
at the music store?

CD.

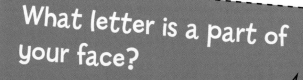

What letter is a part of
your face?

The letter i.

What's the longest
word in the world?

Smiles. Between the first
and last S is a mile.

What letter of the alphabet is blue and flies?

J.

What two letters do you drink for breakfast?

O.J.

Why is the letter T like an island?

It is in the middle of water.

What letters are not in the alphabet?

The ones in the mail!

What did the spelling teacher say to the kid who fell down the stairs?

R-U-O-K?

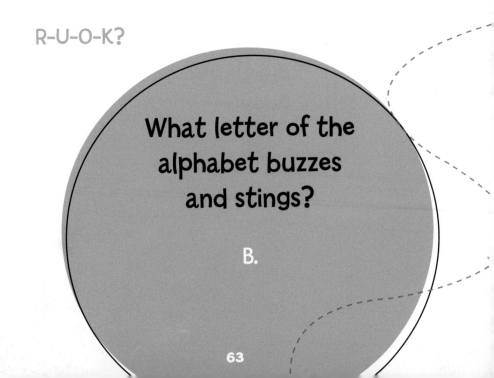

What letter of the alphabet buzzes and stings?

B.

How is the letter S like a slippery floor?

They both make a kid skid!

If the alphabet goes from A-Z, what goes from Z-A?

Zebra.

How is the letter D like a rain gutter?

They both make rain drain.

What 8-letter word has ALL the letters in it?

Alphabet.

What did one math book say to the other math book?

"Man, have I got problems!"

What is the difference between a new penny and an old quarter?

Twenty-four cents.

How are 2+2=5 and your left hand alike?

Neither is right.

What kind of pliers do you use in math class?

Multipliers.

What kind of ant
can count?

An accountant.

From what number can you take
away half and be left with nothing?

The number 8. If you take away the top half,
you have nothing left.

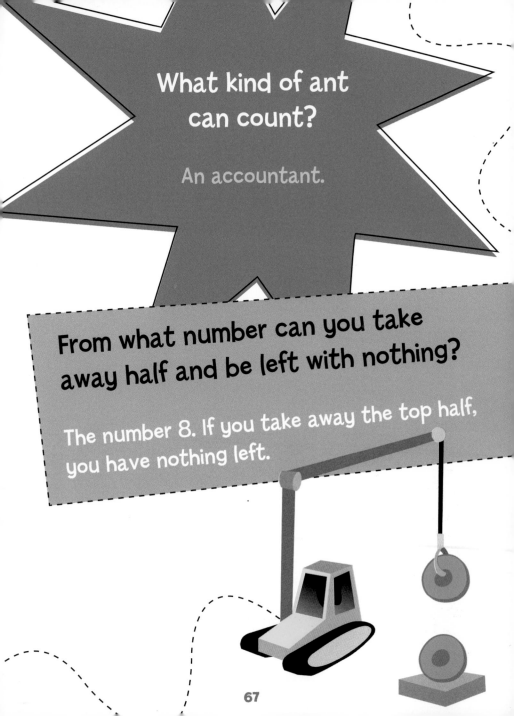

What is a whale's favorite letter?

C.

Why does Lucy like the letter K?

Because it makes Lucy lucky.

What is the coldest letter?

C because it is in the middle of ice.

How many peas are there in a pint?

There is only one P in pint.

How do you spell *cold* with only two letters?

IC.

How do you spell *we* with two letters, but without using the letters W and E?

U and I.

Why is it dangerous to do math in the jungle?

If you add four and four, you get ate.

How do you spell *too much* with two letters?

XS.

Why is the letter A like a flower?

Because a B comes after it.

Why is the letter B hot?

Because it makes oil boil.

What word becomes smaller when you add two letters to it?

Small.

How many letters are there in the alphabet?

Eleven: T-H-E-A-L-P-H-A-B-E-T.

What is in the middle of March?

The letter R.

When you take away two letters from this five-letter word, you get one. What word is it?

Stone.

Why is the number 9
like a peacock?

Because without its tail,
it is nothing.

What kind of tree is a math
teacher's favorite?

Geometry.

What letter can make you very wet?

C.

How much dirt is there in a hole that is 1-foot deep and 1-foot across?

None. A hole is empty.

How can you spell eighty in only two letters?

AT.

Which two letters of the alphabet are nothing?

MT.

What is the center of gravity?

The letter V.

What increases in value when you turn it upside down?

The number 6.

What letter should you avoid?

The letter A because it makes men mean.

What eight-letter word has one letter in it?

Envelope.

Which three letters of the alphabet frighten all criminals?

FBI.

What five-letter word has six left when you take two letters away?

Sixty.

How many feet are in a yard?

It depends how many people are standing in it.

If all the letters of the alphabet were invited to a tea party, which letters would be late?

U, V, W, X, Y, and Z because they all come after T.

How can you say *rabbit* without using the letter R?

Bunny.

Why is six afraid of seven?

Because seven ate nine.

Which word in the dictionary is spelled incorrectly?

Incorrectly.

HOW TO BE FUNNY

KNOCK, KNOCK!

The following tips will help you become rich, famous, and popular. Well, maybe not. However, they will help you tell a good joke.

WHAT TO DO:

- Know the joke.
- Allow suspense to build, but don't drag it out too long.
- Make the punch line clear.
- Be confident, use emotion, and smile.

WHAT NOT TO DO:

- Do not ask your friend over and over if they "get it."
- Do not speak in a different language than your audience.
- Do not tell the same joke every day.
- Do not keep saying, "This joke is so funny!"